APPLE GRUMBLE

For grandmas everywhere,
for everything.
HUW

For Mum, who makes a
mean apple crumble.
BEN

First published in the United Kingdom in 2022 by
Thames & Hudson Ltd, 181A High Holborn, London WC1V 7QX

Apple Grumble © 2022 Thames & Hudson Ltd, London

Concept and Text © 2022 Huw Lewis Jones
Illustration and Design © 2022 Ben Sanders

British Library Cataloguing-in-Publication Data
A catalogue record for this book is available from the British Library

ISBN 978-0-500-65244-2

Printed and bound in Latvia by Livonia Print

Be the first to know about our new releases,
exclusive content and author events by visiting
thamesandhudson.com
thamesandhudsonusa.com
thamesandhudson.com.au

APPLE GRUMBLE

HUW LEWIS JONES
& BEN SANDERS

This is Apple.

He's still a nasty
piece of fruit.

And now he's
grumpy too...

This is Granny Smith,
one of the oldest apples.

Perhaps she can teach
him some manners?

You drank Pea's tea, and stole Cat's hat,
and other naughty things like that.

Apple, it's time you behaved!

But Apple doesn't want
to be nice.

No way.

He's got other plans...

You should be
sweet like us.

Here come Red and Golden.
Two delicious apples.

Teamwork
makes the
dream work.

Here come Bramley,
Braeburn and Cox.
Three popular apples.

It's not cool to
be angry, man.

Here come Honeycrisp,
Gala, Pink Lady and Jazz.
Four fabulous apples.

And here comes Pineapple!

What?
He's not even
an apple.

This book is too crowded
for Apple's taste.

Has he made friends?

Can he be good?

What do you think?

Ten not so happy apples.
(and a pineapple).

One very bad apple.

Bad Apple is happy.
No need to grumble...

...now all the rest
are covered in crumble.

Huw Lewis Jones is a polar-exploring author and historian who lives in Cornwall, UK. His books include *Explorers' Sketchbooks*, *The Writer's Map* and *Archipelago* (all Thames & Hudson).

Ben Sanders is an award-winning illustrator and graphic designer based in Ballarat, Australia. He is the author and illustrator of *I've an Uncle Ivan* and *I Could Wear That Hat!* (both Thames & Hudson Australia).

★★★★★ **THIS BOOK IS AMAZING!**
This is obviously the best book in the world. And Bad Apple is a GENIUS. Seriously. Buy this book today. Or else...
– *Anonymous*

★☆☆☆☆ **DO NOT READ THIS BOOK**
Oh please! Do you really want another story about an awful apple? His manners are appalling. This book will teach you nothing!
– *Granny Smith*